Turtle in July

by **Marilyn Singer**

illustrated by **Jerry Pinkney**

ALADDIN BOOKS

Macmillan Publishing Company   *New York*
Maxwell Macmillan Canada   *Toronto*
Maxwell Macmillan International
New York   Oxford   Singapore   Sydney

First Aladdin Books edition 1994

Aladdin Books   Maxwell Macmillan Canada, Inc.
Macmillan Publishing Company   1200 Eglinton Avenue East
866 Third Avenue   Suite 200
New York, NY 10022   Don Mills, Ontario M3C 3N1

Macmillan Publishing Company is part of the Maxwell Communication Group
of Companies.
Printed in Hong Kong
10   9   8   7   6   5   4   3   2   1
The text of this book is set in 13 point Meridian.
The illustrations are rendered in pen and pencil with watercolor on paper.

Library of Congress Cataloging-in-Publication Data
Singer, Marilyn.
     Turtle in July / by Marilyn Singer ; illustrated by Jerry Pinkney.—1st Aladdin
Books ed.
          p.   cm.
     Summary: An illustrated collection about the activities of particular animals in
each month of the year.
     ISBN 0-689-71805-5
     1. Animals—Juvenile poetry. 2. Months—Juvenile poetry. 3. Children's
poetry, American. [1. Animals—Poetry. 2. Months—Poetry. 3. Seasons—
Poetry. 4. American poetry.] I. Pinkney, Jerry, ill. II. Title.
PS3569.I546T87   1994
811'.54—dc20   93-14430

To Tal, Shanie,

Noa, Yaacov,

and Susan Tuchman

—M.S.

To Rob Howard,

friend and supporter

—J.P.

BULLHEAD IN WINTER

in winter
I sleep
    belly down in the shallows
below me
    mud
above me
    ice
next to me
  on either side
    bullheads asleep
    belly down in the shallows
below them
    mud
above them
    ice
next to them
  on either side
    bullheads asleep
    belly down in the shallows

January Deer

I am a January deer,
so swift and light
the hard-packed snow does not even
   crunch
beneath my hooves.
While others around me
sleep in silent caves,
   I run
through the white world
   with wide-open eyes.

Barn Owl

February night
     (sweep)
Thick clouds
No moon
     (search sweep)
Soft snow
No ice
     (hush sweep)
Patience
Silence
Wait for the
     (sweep)
     squeak
Now swoop
     snatch
     crack
A hard time for owls
But harder still for mice

Deer Mouse

get   get get get   get
  get
    out of the nest
  get
    into the cold
get   get get get
  get
    food
    lots of food
  get
    seeds
    berries
    nuts
    bugs
    bark
get enough to last
get enough to store
get more
get   get get get   get
  get going
    move
      hustle
don't rustle
don't squeak
    beware
    danger in the air
get busy
get done
get   get get get
  get out of here
    run

BULLHEAD IN SPRING

in spring
I spawn
   belly down in the shallows
where no trout
   no whitefish
   no salmon
   can go
I lay
   one two three four
     thousand eggs
my mate and I watch them hatch
                 hatch
   in the warming mud
little black bullheads
   swimming free
    to new mud
     new shallows

March Bear

Who I?
　Where I?
When I now?
　No matter
Need water
Few berries
Fresh ants
　Not so hungry
Or am I?
Don't think so
　Not yet
And anyway it's too early for honey
Funny
That odor
　This river
That hollow
　This den
I know them
　Well, sort of
I've been here
　But when?
　No matter
New morning
Remember it then

april is a dog's dream
the soft grass is growing
the sweet breeze is blowing
the air all full of singing feels just right
so no excuses now
we're going to the park
to chase and charge and chew
and I will make you see
what spring is all about

Myrtle Warblers

Me me me
I am
me me me
See the yellow yellow yellow
    on my wing-ing-ings
Me me me
I am
me me me
I'm the fellow fellow fellow
    here who sing-ing-ings

May May May
It is
May May May
Come and pair up pair up pair up
    you and me me me
May May May
It is
May May May
Meet me there up there up there up
    in that tree tree tree

Hi hi hi
I say
hi hi hi
I think your voice your voice your voice
    is the best best best
Hi hi hi
I say
hi hi hi
You are my choice my choice my choice
    Come, let's nest nest nest

BULLHEAD IN SUMMER

in summer
I eat
    belly down in the mud
  moving slow and easy
I find
      worms
  and water beetles
      pondweed
  and snails
      dragonflies
      alderflies
      crayfish
  and side swimmers
over my head
  a turtle passes by
I don't bother him
he doesn't bother me
  good summer neighbors

Cow

I approve of June
Fresh food to chew
   and chew
   and chew
Lots of room to move around
   or lie down
Not too hot
Not too cold
Not too wet
Not too dry
A good roof of sky over me and my calf
Who's now halfway up
   on new legs
He'll want a meal real soon
Yes, I approve of June

Turtle in July

Heavy
Heavy hot
Heavy hot hangs
Thick sticky
Icky
But I lie
Nose high
Cool pool
No fool
A turtle in July

Dragonfly

Look
  skim
    there
      snap
        eat
Repeat
Look
  skim
    there
      snap
        eat
Repeat
Look
  skim
    there
      snap
        hey
It got away
Look
  skim
    there
      snap
      oh
Where'd that one go?
August slow?
For a dragonfly
        no
Look
  skim
    there
      snap
        eat
Repeat

BULLHEAD IN AUTUMN

in autumn
I settle
    belly down in the shallows
above me
    leaves
      red and yellow
  spinning slowly
    in the wind and water
on the shore
    a lone fisher
      casts a line
  begging me to bite
don't waste your time, fisher
  it's autumn
    and in autumn
I settle
    belly down in the shallows

Timber Rattlesnake

Summer it still is
   Yes
September stones
Warm bones
Warm blood
Strike I still can
    Yes
Snare and swallow the harvesting mouse
               the shuffling rat
But slant they do the sun's rays
Shorter grow the days
    Yes
Soon September stones
Chill bones
Chill blood
Stiff shall I grow
And so below I'll slide
Beneath stones
Beneath soil
Coil I still can
    Yes
Sleep safe
Sleep sound
Snake underground

Canada Goose

Did I tell you?
I should tell you
Going home
We're going home
Are you coming?
Yes, you're coming
Going home
We're going home
How the sun will warm each feather
How the wind will make us fly
Follow me—I'll be your leader
As we flap across the sky
Are you ready?
I am ready
Going home
We're going home
Is it time now?
It is time now
October's happened
And we're going home

Beavers in November

This stick   here
That stick   there
  Mud, more mud, add mud, good mud
That stick   here
This stick   there
  Mud, more mud, add mud, good mud
    You pat
    I gnaw
    I pile
    You store
This stick   here
That stick   there
  Mud, more mud, add mud, good mud
    You guard
    I pack
    I dig
    You stack
That stick   here
This stick   there
  Mud, more mud, add mud, good mud
    I trim
    You mold
    To keep
    Out cold
This stick   here
That stick   there
  Mud, more mud, add mud, good mud

Cat

I prefer
warm fur,
a perfect fire
to lie beside,
a cozy lap
where I can nap,
an empty chair
when she's not there.
I want heat
  on my feet
   on my nose
    on my hide.
No cat I remember
dislikes December
  inside.